A Note to Parents and Caregivers:

Read-it! Readers are for children who are just starting on the amazing road to reading. These beautiful books support both the acquisition of reading skills and the love of books.

The PURPLE LEVEL presents basic topics and objects using high frequency words and simple language patterns.

The RED LEVEL presents familiar topics using common words and repeating sentence patterns.

The BLUE LEVEL presents new ideas using a larger vocabulary and varied sentence structure.

The YELLOW LEVEL presents more challenging ideas, a broad vocabulary, and wide variety in sentence structure.

The GREEN LEVEL presents more complex ideas, an extended vocabulary range, and expanded language structures.

The ORANGE LEVEL presents a wide range of ideas and concepts using challenging vocabulary and complex language structures.

When sharing a book with your child, read in short stretches, pausing often to talk about the pictures. Have your child turn the pages and point to the pictures and familiar words. And be sure to reread favorite stories or parts of stories.

There is no right or wrong way to share books with children. Find time to read with your child, and pass on the legacy of literacy.

Adria F. Klein, Ph.D.
Professor Emeritus
California State University
San Bernardino, California

Editor: Christianne Jones
Page Production: Melissa Kes/JoAnne Nelson
Art Director: Keith Griffin
Managing Editor: Catherine Neitge
Editorial Consultant: Mary Lindeen
The illustrations in this book were done in watercolor.

Picture Window Books
5115 Excelsior Boulevard
Suite 232
Minneapolis, MN 55416
877-845-8392
www.picturewindowbooks.com

Printed in the United States of America.

Library of Congress Cataloging-in-Publication Data
Williams, Jacklyn.
Happy Valentine's Day, Gus! / by Jacklyn Williams ; illustrated by Doug Cushman.
p. cm. — (Read-it! readers. Gus the hedgehog)
Summary: Every time Gus has a lovely Valentine's gift for his mother, it seems to
meet with disaster.
ISBN 1-4048-0962-7 (hardcover)
[1. Valentine's Day—Fiction. 2. Mothers—Fiction. 3. Gifts—Fiction. 4. Hedgehogs—
Fiction.] I. Cushman, Doug, ill. II. Title. III. Series.

PZ7.W6656Hav 2004
[E]—dc22   2004023315

Happy Valentine's Day, Gus!

By Jacklyn Williams

Illustrated by Doug Cushman

Special thanks to our advisers for their expertise:

Adria F. Klein, Ph.D.
Professor Emeritus, California State University
San Bernardino, California

Susan Kesselring, M.A.
Literacy Educator
Rosemount-Apple Valley-Eagan (Minnesota) School District

PiCTURE WiNDOW BOOKS
Minneapolis, Minnesota

It was just another Friday at school until
the teacher pulled the box of art supplies
out of the closet.

"We're going to spend the rest of the afternoon making cards for Valentine's Day," she said.

Gus could hardly wait to get started.
He wanted to give his mother the most
beautiful card ever.

First, he poured glue on a lacy white heart.

Then, he poured glue on a shiny red heart.

Gus pushed the two together and wrote:

"Mom, you mean more to me than eating ice cream or climbing a tree! BE MY VALENTINE!"

Mom, you mean more to me than eating ice cream or climbing a tree! BE MY VALENTINE!

Just as Gus finished, the final bell rang.
Gus and Bean raced out of the door and onto
the bus. Billy plopped down in the seat behind
them. Bean tugged at Gus's card.

"Let me see it," Bean said.

"No, let me see it," Billy said, as he snatched the card away from Gus.

"Give it back!" Gus demanded.

Just then, a big gust of wind blew through the
open window. The card sailed out the window
and down the street.

"STOP THE BUS!" shouted Gus.

But the bus did not stop. It kept heading north, while Gus's card headed south.

Gus spent Saturday morning worrying.
He flopped down on his bed.

"What am I going to do?" he asked Bean.
"My mom's card must be halfway to the
moon by now."

"So, buy another one," said Bean.

Gus held up his piggy bank, closed one eye, and looked into the slit with the other. Then he shook the piggy bank back and forth as hard as he could. Nickels, dimes, and quarters rained down on his bed.

"Jackpot!" Gus yelled. "Let's go to the store."

Gus and Bean looked at a lot of gifts at
the store.

"Candy is a better present than a card,"
said Bean. "But we should try a piece before you
give it to your mom, just to make sure it tastes all
right."

"Maybe you're right," said Gus. "But just one."

Gus handed Bean a Chocolate Buster Cluster, then tossed one into his own mouth. He closed the lid tight and tucked the box under his arm. An hour later, Gus and Bean walked out of the store with a half-eaten box of chocolates.

As Gus and Bean headed home, they heard
Billy. He was zigzagging down the sidewalk,
heading straight for Gus.

"Out of my way!" Billy hollered.

"Watch out!" Gus hollered back.

16

Too late! Gus flew one way, and the candy flew another. The gift was ruined.

"Now what?" Gus asked Bean.

"You'll think of something," Bean answered.

"I just thought of something," said Gus.
"I could make my mom a bunch of
flowers. I just need some colored paper."

"I have a lot of paper," said Bean. "Let's go
over to my house."

Gus sat down at Bean's desk. In front of him lay a stack of colorful paper. He took out a piece of yellow paper and a bottle cap. He laid the bottle cap on the paper and traced around it.

Next, he got some sheets of bright green paper.

He rolled them up, one at a time,

until he had three tubes that looked like

flower stems.

After that, he got a pair of scissors, some white paper, and a bottle of glue. Cut, cut, cut. Glue, glue, glue. Before long, Gus had made three beautiful flowers. He held them up.

"Perfect!" he exclaimed.

Just as Gus headed for home, rain clouds
started to gather. Lightning streaked across the
sky. Thunder rumbled. First, only a few drops
fell. Soon, more and more drops fell.

"Run!" hollered Bean.

By the time Gus reached his front door,
he was soaked—so were his flowers.

"I give up," sighed Gus.

Valentine's Day finally came. It was time for giving presents and going to the town's annual Valentine's party. Gus was not happy.

He had his special clothes for the party.
He had his special shoes for the party.
But he didn't have his special present
for his mom.

Gus's mom had bought a new pair of shoes. Her favorite dress was washed and hanging up to dry. She'd put Gus's present away in a secret hiding place. She was ready. But Gus was not ready. What was he going to do?

Gus went down to the basement. He sat on a stool to think. The stool wobbled back and forth, and so did Gus's thoughts.

"No supplies to make a card. No money to buy candy. No time to make any more flowers," Gus sighed.

27

The stool kept on wobbling, and so did Gus's thoughts. Suddenly, he jumped to his feet.

"I've got it!" he said. "I'll fix the legs on this old stool and paint it to look brand new. Mom will be so surprised!"

Gus picked up a brush and began to paint. Mom's voice floated down the stairs.

"Gus, are you down there?" she asked.

Panicked, Gus grabbed the nearest thing he could find, threw it over the stool, and plopped down. He soon realized he had grabbed his mom's favorite dress.

"I made a mess of everything," sniffed Gus.
"I lost your card. I dropped your candy. I got
your flowers wet. I even wrecked your stool.
Worst of all, I ruined your favorite dress."

"Ruined it?" she said. "It's the best Valentine's dress I've ever had!"

She gave Gus a great big hug.

"Now, let's get ready for our date," she said.

More *Read-it!* Readers

Bright pictures and fun stories help you practice your reading skills. Look for more books at your level.

GUS THE HEDGEHOG

Happy Easter, Gus! by Jacklyn Williams

Happy Halloween, Gus! by Jacklyn Williams

Happy Valentine's Day, Gus! by Jacklyn Williams

Merry Christmas, Gus! by Jacklyn Williams

Looking for a specific title or level?
A complete list of *Read-it!* Readers is available on our
Web site: *www.picturewindowbooks.com*

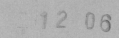